The Red Ghost

by *Marion Dane Bauer*

illustrated by *Peter Ferguson*

A STEPPING STONE BOOK™
Random House New York

To Taylor and Katrina—M.D.B.

To Hannah and Robert,
who know what's hiding in the closet—P.F.

Text copyright © 2008 by Marion Dane Bauer
Illustrations copyright © 2008 by Peter Ferguson

Visit us on the Web!
www.steppingstonesbooks.com
www.randomhouse.com/kids

Educators and librarians, for a variety of teaching tools, visit us at
www.randomhouse.com/teachers

Library of Congress Cataloging-in-Publication Data
Bauer, Marion Dane.
The red ghost / by Marion Dane Bauer ; illustrated by Peter Ferguson. — 1st ed.
   p.   cm.
"A Stepping Stone book."
Summary: When Jenna gives her little sister an old doll in red velvet as a birthday present, some very disturbing instances occur and Jenna begins to suspect that the doll might be haunted.
ISBN 978-0-375-84081-4 (trade hardcover) — ISBN 978-0-375-94081-1 (lib. bdg.) — ISBN 978-0-375-84082-1 (pbk.)
[1. Dolls—Fiction. 2. Spirit possession—Fiction. 3. Supernatural—Fiction.
4. Sisters—Fiction.] I. Ferguson, Peter, ill. II. Title.
PZ7.B3262Re 2008   [Fic]—dc22   2007010354

Printed in the United States of America
10 9 8 7 6 5 4 3 2 1
First Edition

Contents

1

A Birthday Present
for Quinn

The doll wore red velvet. Her dress was made of red velvet and her bonnet was, too. Both were trimmed in white lace, but the white lace only made the velvet seem more red.

Jenna had found the doll on a table at Miss Tate's garage sale. Dishes, stacks of old magazines, candles, even a couple of mouse-traps lay around her. All of it was junk, really. Except for the doll.

Jenna couldn't take her eyes off the doll.

"Look," she said to her friend Dallas. "Isn't she pretty?" She pointed but didn't touch.

"Wow! That thing looks really old!" Dallas grabbed the doll off the table. She held it out at arm's length.

That was just like Dallas. The doll did look old . . . and fragile. Jenna hadn't dared pick it up. What if Miss Tate objected? But Dallas didn't worry about those things. She just did them and then seemed surprised when she got into trouble.

Jenna moved closer to inspect the doll. She had painted-on hair, round cheeks, dimples in the backs of her chubby hands. She had real eyelashes, too.

"Are you still into dolls?" Dallas asked. Anyone would know at a glance that *Dallas* wasn't "into dolls." She wore her usual summer outfit—ragged cutoffs and a baseball cap turned backward on her head.

Jenna made a face at Dallas's question. Dallas knew better. Jenna had played with dolls when she was little, but she was going into the fourth grade now. "It's Quinn's birthday next week," she said. "And you know how she loves dolls."

Quinn was Jenna's little sister, and Jenna hadn't found a birthday present for her yet. The truth was she hadn't saved enough of her allowance to buy much of anything.

"I wonder how much Miss Tate wants for it," Dallas said.

Jenna shrugged. "Too much probably. She looks valuable."

"It looks *old*," Dallas corrected.

"Well, old things can be valuable. When they get really old, they're called antiques," Jenna said.

"I'm not an antique!"

Jenna jumped.

Miss Tate had come up behind them. "But you're right," she said. "That doll is old. It used to belong to my little sister, so it's almost as old as I am. But that doesn't make it an antique, either."

Jenna didn't know what to say. As usual, though, Dallas did. "How much do you want for it?" she asked. "Jenna wants to buy it for Quinn."

Is that what I want? Jenna wondered. And even if it was, what made Dallas think she could afford it?

Miss Tate was tall and very skinny, kind of like a pole with a puff of white hair on top. She crossed her arms over her flat front and frowned at the doll.

"For her birthday," Jenna told her. "Next week she'll be five."

"Five years old? That little tyke?" Miss Tate's face rumpled into a smile. "Well, in that case, you can have it for Quinn. No charge."

"Really?" Jenna couldn't believe her luck. She had found a birthday present for Quinn. And it wasn't going to cost her a cent!

Miss Tate gave an emphatic nod. "I should have gotten rid of that doll a long time ago," she said. "I never did like it."

Jenna wondered how anyone could not like such a pretty doll. Still, she wasn't going to argue. She said only, "Thank you, Miss Tate!" She took the doll from Dallas and gave it a squeeze. The head and arms and legs were hard, but the body was soft and huggable.

"Don't thank *me*," Miss Tate said. "It was my mama who insisted on keeping the thing." And she turned abruptly and became very busy straightening a stack of *National Geographic*s.

"Thank you so much," Jenna repeated anyway.

And Dallas added, "Quinn is going to love—"

But Miss Tate interrupted. "Run along now, girls." She picked up the stack of magazines and carried them to another table. She spoke without looking back. "And take that silly doll with you. It's high time it was out of my attic."

Jenna and Dallas looked at each other and shrugged. Who knew why their neighbor was suddenly so cross? Sometimes it was hard to figure grown-ups.

"Let's go to my house first," Dallas said. "We'll gift-wrap the doll before you take it home. Then Quinn won't see it and spoil the surprise."

Jenna gave the red-velvet doll another squeeze and followed Dallas across the street. Wasn't this lucky? A birthday present for her little sister. An absolutely free birthday present.

And Quinn was sure to love it!

2
Ftt-t-t-t-t!

Jenna and Dallas couldn't find gift wrap at Dallas's house. The best they could do were the comics from last Sunday's paper. But the comics were colorful, and Quinn wouldn't care. She was a package ripper, anyway. She never stopped to admire the wrapping, no matter how pretty it was.

Dallas spread the comics out on the table. Jenna held the doll and gazed into her eyes. "There's something about this doll's eyes," she said to Dallas. "They're so . . ." She searched for the word.

"Blue," Dallas supplied.

Jenna looked closer. Yes, the doll's eyes were blue. They were a sunburst of different shades of blue. But that wasn't what she had meant to say. What made her study the eyes had nothing to do with their color.

She tipped the doll back. The eyes closed with a small clunk. She righted her again. They snapped open. When she tipped the doll sideways, the eyes rolled to one side. The doll peered back at Jenna as if she were saying, *What do you think you're doing, anyway?*

"It's not the color," Jenna said at last.

"Her eyes look sad . . . or angry. Or . . . I'm not sure what it is."

Dallas laughed. "Woo-o-o-o! Woo-o-o-o!" She fluttered her fingers in front of Jenna's face. "I'll bet Miss Tate's old doll is haunted!"

Jenna didn't respond. She just laid the doll down on the paper. She and Dallas had been friends as long as she could remember, but sometimes the girl could be annoying.

Jenna folded the newspaper over the doll, covering her eyes. They were closed now, anyway. "It's just a feeling," she said. "I know it's silly."

Dallas and Jenna both worked at taping the package. It took lots of tape. The doll was an odd shape. A hand or a foot or a snub nose seemed to poke back out every time they had the package closed.

When they were done, Jenna tucked the gift under her arm. They headed next door to her house. The moment they stepped through the door, Quinn appeared. "What's that?" she asked. She pointed at the package.

"That's for us to know and you to find out," Dallas tossed back.

It wasn't the smartest answer to give Quinn. She was the kind of little kid who refused to be left out of anything. Jenna could be scooping poop out of the cat's litter box, and Quinn would be at her elbow. A secret package was going to be too much for her to bear.

Jenna thought fast. "It's just some garbage Dallas's mom asked us to throw away." She ducked down the hall toward her room.

"Then why are you taking it to your room?" Quinn yelled after her.

That was a fair enough question. Why was she taking garbage to her room?

"Because she's got a trash can in there. Didn't you know?" Dallas called back.

Quinn followed them to the door of Jenna's room. "Don't you have trash cans at your house?" she asked.

"No," Dallas said, shutting the door firmly in Quinn's face.

The two girls looked at one another and collapsed into giggles. Jenna couldn't help laughing, even though she knew Quinn could hear. She also knew that nothing made Quinn madder than being laughed at.

"Jen-n-n-n-a!" Quinn wailed.

Jenna ignored her. She leaned the lumpy package against her pillow. Then she stepped back to study it.

Their black-and-white cat, Rocco, lay

asleep in his usual spot at the foot of Jenna's bed. He was curled into a tight ball, his nose tucked beneath his tail.

"The package needs something," Jenna said. "Ribbon, I think."

Dallas nodded. "That would help," she said. "It's not exactly—"

But before Dallas could finish saying what the package wasn't exactly, Rocco came to life. He woke as if he'd been poked with a sharp stick.

Ftt-t-t-t-t!

He jumped to his feet, spitting. The fur along his spine bristled. His tail puffed like a bottlebrush. And all this sudden fury was directed at the lumpy package!

"Hey!" Jenna said. "Take it easy, Rocco."

But Rocco wasn't going to take it easy. He danced over to the package on the tips of his toes and took a swipe at it. Then he leapt off the bed and streaked for the door.

Dallas opened the door just in time for Rocco to make his exit. He whizzed down the hall.

Quinn still stood on the other side.

"What's wrong with Rocco?" she asked. But she wasn't looking at Rocco. She was looking at the package on the bed.

"Don't know," Dallas replied. "You'd better go see." She closed the door again.

Both girls stared at the package. An eye stared back at them from behind the slit Rocco's claws had made in the paper.

"It looks like Rocco has it in for Miss Tate's old doll," Dallas said.

"Yeah. I guess so." Jenna sat down next to the torn package. Her knees were suddenly wobbly.

What had gotten into Rocco? He was ordinarily a very gentle cat. She had never seen him attack anything fiercer than a buzzing fly.

The truth was, though, it wasn't Rocco that was scaring her.

3

"Did You Hear That?"

"We'll have to get more tape." Jenna said it calmly, as though having Rocco go crazy wasn't the least bit strange. But her legs still felt weak.

Dallas poked at the long slit in the paper. "Either that or start over with new paper."

"I'll get tape," Jenna said.

She didn't know why exactly, but she didn't want to unwrap the doll. She'd just keep her covered until she gave her to Quinn.

When Jenna opened the door, Quinn no longer waited on the other side.

Jenna found tape and a bow, too, in the hall closet. When she got back to the room, Dallas stood frowning at the package.

"Anything wrong?" Jenna asked.

"Of course not," Dallas snapped.

Jenna gave Dallas a long look. Why was she so cross?

Jenna looked down at the blue eye peering through the tear in the paper. The eye seemed to be accusing her of something. But what? She wasn't doing anything bad to the doll. Just wrapping it. And it certainly wasn't *her* fault that Rocco had gone crazy.

Quickly, Jenna stretched several layers of

tape over the slit. Then she put the red stick-on bow over that. The bow was left over from Christmas. It was red velvet like the doll's dress.

"There," she said.

Dallas had been watching without offering to help. "Now put it away," she ordered.

"Why?" Jenna asked. She was beginning to feel a bit annoyed again. Dallas could be *so* bossy. "It's all wrapped. Quinn won't know what it is."

"But Rocco will still hate it," Dallas said. "Cats have some kind of extra sense, don't you think? And who knows what he'll do if he sees the package again?"

Jenna shrugged. "Okay." She picked up the gift and tucked it under her bed.

"No!" Dallas practically shouted.

"No?" Jenna turned to stare at her.

"You don't want that thing under your bed," Dallas told her. "That's not a good idea at all. Just think about it under your bed staring up at you. Right through the mattress. All night long!"

Jenna laughed. "This is a doll, Dallas. Remember?"

But Dallas wasn't laughing. "You need to put it away. Really away. How about your closet?"

Jenna shrugged. "Okay," she said. There was no point in arguing. When Dallas got an idea into her head, she didn't let go of it easily. And Jenna wasn't even going to ask what Dallas was thinking now.

Jenna put the package on the shelf in the back of her closet. She shut the door.

"Do you think it will stay there?" Dallas asked.

Jenna laughed again. "Do you think she's going to get up and walk away?" She flopped down on her bed.

"Who knows?" Dallas said.

Jenna studied her friend's face. Was she joking? But she looked completely serious. So Jenna just asked, "What do you want to do next?"

Dallas shrugged. "Let's go back to my house."

"Okay." Jenna sat up. She still didn't know what was going on. Dallas usually liked to play at Jenna's house. She had two little brothers at home who were always in the way.

But they had no more than started down the hall when Dallas stopped. "Did you hear that?"

"Hear what?"

Dallas tipped her head. "That!" she repeated. "It's like a . . . a voice from far away. Like someone calling."

Jenna listened, too, but she heard nothing. She couldn't even hear Quinn off complaining to their mother . . . which was what she was probably doing.

Jenna shook her head. "I don't hear a thing," she said.

"You're sure?" Dallas asked.

"Positive."

Dallas listened again, then gave a small shudder. "Let's get out of here," she said.

Jenna followed Dallas. But she couldn't help wondering. What could there possibly be to hear?

4
From the Closet

Jenna woke in the middle of the night. At least she thought it must be the middle of the night. Her room was completely dark. The house was silent. The only light she could see snuck through her window from the street-lamp on the corner.

The streetlamp didn't really light her room. Mostly it just made shadows.

She lay still for a few moments. Why was

she awake? Why was her heart pounding? Maybe she'd had a bad dream. She couldn't remember any dream, though.

But then she heard something. Was that what had wakened her? She held her breath. The sound was so faint it was almost like no sound at all.

What was it?

It sounded like paper rattling. Who could be rattling paper in her room in the middle of the night? Mice?

And then there was that other sound . . . very low, almost impossible to make out.

Was it someone crying?

She pushed her blanket aside and stood up. Was Quinn crying? That wasn't very likely. Quinn rarely cried.

Besides, Quinn's room was right next to hers. If she were crying, she wouldn't sound so far away.

Still, Jenna decided to check.

She padded across her room and down the hall. She stopped in her sister's open doorway.

Quinn's room was closer to the front of the house, so the streetlamp shone brighter

here. Jenna could make out her little sister sprawled on her bed. She held her Raggedy Ann in the crook of her arm. Quinn loved that doll. She had hauled it around with her until it was flat.

Quinn's breathing was steady and quiet. She wasn't crying. She wasn't even whimpering. She was sleeping. That was all.

Jenna went back to her room. She paused just inside her door to listen again. She heard only silence. Absolute silence.

She climbed back into bed. She pulled the blanket up to her chin, rolled over, and closed her eyes.

She was just drifting toward sleep when she heard it again. A distinct rustle and a low sound like a sob.

Even as her arms pricked into goose bumps, Jenna figured it out. It was Rocco. Who else?

Their cat had gotten shut in her closet. That happened sometimes. He liked hidden places. Every time anyone opened a door, he scooted through to explore. And sometimes he got shut in . . . in closets, kitchen cupboards, the laundry room. Once he even got shut inside the TV cabinet. He'd made a mess of the DVDs before Dad found him and let him out.

This time he must be in her closet!

Jenna pushed the blanket back again. She swung her feet out of the bed. But she stopped before she stood up. She just stopped and sat there, thinking.

The doll was in her closet, too. Miss Tate's doll. The one she was going to give to Quinn. It was all wrapped up, taped up, even decorated with a red bow. But it was in there.

And suddenly Jenna didn't want to open the closet door.

Not in the middle of the night with the streetlamp stretching shadows across her room. Not with the sounds—the rustling, the crying—growing louder.

Rocco was in her closet. Those sounds were only her cat. She was certain of that.

But still . . .

Jenna lay back down. It wouldn't hurt Rocco to wait until morning to get out. Maybe he'd learn to pay more attention if he had to wait. He shouldn't crawl into places where he could get shut in, anyway.

Besides, the sounds had grown quieter now. So quiet she could hardly hear them. And then she couldn't hear them at all.

Her room was just as silent as the rest of the house. It was silent with sleep. Rocco must have gone to sleep, too.

• • •

When she awoke the next morning, the first thing Jenna remembered was that Rocco was trapped in her closet. She sat up quickly and looked at the closet door. It was closed, as it had been last night. It was tightly closed, and all was quiet.

Then she drew in her breath. At the bottom of her bed lay Rocco, curled into a familiar black-and-white ball. He was sleeping peacefully. He was even snoring just a bit.

So what had she heard last night in her closet?

And what was it Dallas thought she had heard yesterday?

Jenna reached for her clothes. She had to go talk to Dallas!

5

"Already Full"

Dallas looked up from her bowl of Cheerios. "Tell me again what it sounded like," she said.

"I don't know!" The truth was Jenna didn't want to say it again. She knew what she had heard last night. Now, though, with the morning sun spilling across Dallas's kitchen table, saying it sounded silly. So she said instead, "Tell me what you heard yesterday . . . when we were leaving the house."

"Nothing," Dallas said. She stirred her Cheerios so hard that the milk sloshed out of the bowl. "I didn't hear anything."

Yes, you did! Jenna wanted to say. But she knew Dallas just didn't want to say it, either. So she took a deep breath and said it herself. "What I heard was like paper rattling. Like someone crying."

"What did the someone say?" Dallas asked.

Jenna shrugged. "Nothing. It was just a voice . . . that's all. No words. I thought it was Rocco."

"But it wasn't Rocco." Dallas picked up a spoonful of Cheerios. She held it in the air in front of her mouth. "Rocco was on your bed this morning."

"And the closet door was still closed," Jenna pointed out.

Dallas plopped the spoon back in the bowl. "We've got to get rid of that doll," she announced. "Right now."

Irritation fizzed through Jenna's veins. She had come to see Dallas because she wanted to talk about what happened. But she hadn't asked Dallas to take over.

"I don't want to get rid of the doll," she said. "What would I give Quinn for her birthday?"

Dallas's eyebrows lifted until they disappeared under her backward-turned cap. "What do you want to do, then?"

"I . . ." But Jenna didn't know what she wanted to do. All she knew was that she didn't want to spend another night with that thing in her closet.

"I know!" Dallas clapped her hands. "Let's give the doll to Quinn this morning. It can still be a birthday present. Just a little early."

Jenna ignored the "let's." Dallas acted as if the doll were a gift from her, too. But it didn't matter who gave Quinn the doll. It was still a great idea. And Dallas could come with her to get the doll out of the closet. Then she wouldn't even mind if Quinn thought it was a gift from both of them.

It wasn't that she really thought a doll was a threat, of course. She just didn't feel like getting her out of the closet by herself. That was all.

"Come on," she said.

The girls found Quinn in her room, playing with Raggedy Ann and a Barbie. It was an odd combination, but that didn't seem to bother Quinn.

"This is for you!" Jenna said, holding up the package wrapped in newspaper comics. "It's a birthday present," she added. She hoped Quinn would like it.

Quinn got to her feet, slowly. She looked confused. "What is it?" she asked. She made no move to take the gift.

"What difference does it make what it is?" Jenna asked.

"It's a birthday present for you!" Dallas reminded her.

Quinn shook her head. "It's not my birthday yet."

Jenna sighed. What was Quinn's problem? "I know it's a little early. But if we give it to you now, you can start playing with it."

Quinn's hands stayed behind her back. "How come it's wrapped so funny?" she asked.

"Because we couldn't find any gift wrap," Dallas told her. She sounded as impatient as Jenna felt.

"We thought you wouldn't mind," Jenna

added. She said it in a way that told Quinn she wasn't supposed to mind.

Quinn's hands came out from behind her back. She took the package from Jenna. She sat down on her bed and tugged at the tape. She pulled at it slowly . . . very slowly. And this was the girl who usually sent gift wrap flying in every direction! Now she couldn't have possibly taken more care.

When at last Quinn pulled the doll out of the newspaper, she held it up. She stared, long and hard. The red-velvet doll stared back.

Suddenly Quinn rose and thrust the doll into Jenna's hands. "Here," she said.

"But it's for you," Jenna told her.

"Isn't she pretty?" Dallas said.

Quinn took a step back. She said, "No!"

"No?" Jenna repeated, astonished. "What do you mean?"

Quinn shook her head violently. "No, I mean . . . thank you. She's pretty. But I don't want her."

"Why not?" Dallas asked. "Is it because she's old? She's practically an antique, you know." Dallas sounded irritated. Jenna was irritated, too.

"Being old makes her special." Jenna held the doll up so Quinn would see how special she was. "I bought her from Miss Tate." The lie made her cheeks go warm. But what did it matter that she hadn't paid any money for the doll? At least it was true that she had gotten her from Miss Tate. "She used to belong to Miss Tate's little sister."

Quinn studied the doll from a careful distance. "I guess that's why she's full," she said.

"Full? What are you talking about?" Jenna's cheeks grew warmer, but it wasn't embarrassment warming her face now. It was pure anger. She couldn't believe Quinn was refusing her gift! And she couldn't imagine what her little sister was talking about. How could a doll be full?

Quinn plopped down on the floor with her other dolls. She held up Raggedy Ann, who stared at them with blank button eyes. "I like my dolls empty," Quinn told them. She said it slowly, as if explaining the obvious to someone who wasn't very bright. "If they're empty, I can pretend. But"—she pointed to the doll in Jenna's hands—"that one's already full."

"Full of what?" Dallas and Jenna asked together.

Quinn shrugged. "I don't know. She just is. I can tell."

6

"The Answer Is No"

"There's only one thing to do," Dallas announced.

Jenna waited. At this point, she didn't care if Dallas took over. If Dallas had an idea—any idea at all—Jenna was ready to hear it.

"We'll give the doll back to Miss Tate," Dallas said.

Of course! Jenna was delighted. Why

hadn't she come up with that herself? It was the perfect solution. She would just tell Miss Tate that her sister didn't want the doll. She would tell her that Quinn said the doll was "full." That would give Miss Tate a good laugh. Little kids could be so funny!

Jenna picked the doll up and smoothed her velvet dress. It was a shame Quinn didn't want her. She was one of the prettiest dolls Jenna had ever seen.

"Come on," Dallas said. She had already started for the door.

Jenna followed.

Miss Tate's garage sale was over, but that didn't matter. She could put the doll back in her attic. Or she could give it to some other little girl. It wouldn't be very hard to find someone whose imagination wasn't as odd as Quinn's.

Dallas walked up to Miss Tate's door first and rang the bell.

Jenna looked down at the doll in her arms. The doll looked back at her. There *was* something odd about those blue eyes, that was for sure. Jenna wouldn't be sorry to see the thing go.

The door opened, and tall, skinny Miss Tate stood in the doorway. She wasn't looking at them, though. She was staring at the doll.

Jenna waited for Dallas to explain, but Dallas stepped aside. Jenna was on her own.

"Uh . . . ," Jenna said. "I brought your doll back."

"I told you. It's not *my* doll," Miss Tate said. She sounded a bit cross.

Jenna didn't know what to say to that. She looked at Dallas, who didn't seem to know, either. "But she was in *your* garage sale. And you gave her to us."

Miss Tate nodded. At least she agreed with that.

"You said I could have her for Quinn . . . for her birthday," Jenna went on.

Again Miss Tate nodded.

Jenna took a deep breath. "Well, I gave her to Quinn, but Quinn doesn't want her."

"She says she's full," Dallas added.

"Full of what?" Miss Tate asked.

But Jenna could only shrug. Dallas did, too. Who knew?

Miss Tate sighed. She stepped out onto the porch and pulled the door shut behind her. You would think she was afraid the girls would dash inside and drop the doll in her house. Or throw the thing past her like a football.

She didn't say anything more, just stood there with her arms crossed in that way she had.

"Maybe your sister would like to have her back," Jenna suggested.

Miss Tate shook her head no. "My sister's dead," she told them.

"Oh," Jenna replied. And then she said, "I'm sorry." That's what she'd heard her mother say when someone died. *I'm sorry.* As though she were apologizing.

But Miss Tate shook her head again. "She died a long time ago. Hazel was just a little girl," she said. "Scarlet fever."

"Oh," Jenna said again. Did you say you were sorry when someone had been dead for a long time?

"She loved that doll," Miss Tate continued. "She slept with it every night. She carried it everywhere."

"And you've kept it ever since she died?" Jenna asked.

"I didn't keep it!" Miss Tate spoke sharply. "My mother was the one. She used to sit and rock that thing all day long . . . all night, too. Like she was rocking Hazel. Everybody told her she had to burn it, but she wouldn't listen."

Dallas, at last, found something to say. "Burn it? Why was she supposed to burn it?"

"It's what you did with scarlet fever," Miss Tate explained. "It was supposed to protect the other children. Back then no one knew what caused it. The sickness just popped up here and there without warning. They thought it must be germs carried on toys, on bedding. So they burned everything. Mama did, too. Everything Hazel had touched—except for that doll."

"Didn't she care that you might get sick?" Jenna asked.

"No." Miss Tate's voice was sharp. "She didn't seem to care about anybody except Hazel. And when Hazel was gone, she cared about that silly doll instead."

Miss Tate's eyes narrowed. "Mama even made a new dress for it . . . just like one she'd made for Hazel. The same bright red velvet. It's what Hazel wanted, though she looked terrible in red. She was a carrot-top, you know. Carrot-tops shouldn't wear red. Even I knew that."

She pursed her lips and glared at the girls. She acted as though all that had happened so long ago was their fault.

Jenna said nothing. What was there to say?

"Her skin was all red splotches from the fever, too," Miss Tate went on. "But that's how Mama dressed her, even for the funeral. In red velvet, no less."

Jenna looked down at the doll in her

arms, at the red-velvet dress, the red-velvet bonnet.

Miss Tate was looking at it, too. Her look was fierce. "Mama wouldn't let anybody else touch that doll. Not even me. Especially not me. For years and years, she kept it on her bed. She held it when she rocked in her chair. All the years I took care of Mama, that doll stayed close beside her. She even talked to it . . . like she was still talking to Hazel."

Miss Tate took a deep breath. "The day Mama died, I put the thing away in the attic," she said. "Yesterday I remembered it was there. I decided it was time for it to go."

She turned away and opened her door. She spoke with her back to them. "So if you want me to take it, the answer is no. I don't care what Quinn says that doll is full of. I don't want it in my house. Do whatever you like with it. I won't have it here again."

And she went inside and slammed the door.

1
A Solution

Jenna and Dallas stood on Miss Tate's porch. Their mouths were open, but neither spoke. What were they supposed to do now?

Dallas finally broke the silence. "Do you have any other ideas?" she asked.

Jenna shook her head. She didn't have another idea in the world. All she knew was that she wasn't going to keep this thing in her closet another night!

She started down the steps. "We could give it to your brothers," she said. Dallas's little brothers were rough. They didn't play with toys. They destroyed them.

"To use for target practice?" Dallas asked. She followed Jenna.

Jenna shrugged. "Sure, if that's what they want to do. Why should we care? Miss Tate doesn't want the thing. She hates it."

But Dallas shook her head. "No way. I don't want it at my house, either."

Jenna didn't argue. She didn't really want to see the fragile old doll in the boys' hands, anyway. If something bad was going to happen to it, she didn't want to have to look at it afterward.

Jenna and Dallas crossed the street. As

they approached Jenna's house, Jenna saw it. Right in front of them. It was the perfect solution. She would never have to see the doll again!

"Hey!" she said. She put a hand on Dallas's arm. "What do you think of *that* for an idea?" She nodded toward the large plastic garbage can at the curb. Dad had set it out for trash day.

"What do I think . . . ?" Dallas frowned at the garbage can. When she looked at Jenna again, her eyes were wide. "You can't be serious!"

"Why not?" Jenna marched up to the can. She lifted the lid. It was full of white plastic bags fat with garbage. The one on top had split. Some stuff poked through.

She looked back at Dallas to see what she would say.

Dallas pulled off her baseball cap and pushed her hair back. She settled the cap on her head again. "You're going to throw Miss Tate's doll in the garbage?" she asked. "Really?"

"Of course!" Jenna said it cheerfully, as though she threw away dolls every day.

"Well . . . okay." Dallas shrugged. "I guess." She came closer and peered into the can, too. "I mean . . . why not?"

Dallas was right. Why not? Jenna pressed down the top bag to make more room.

"Nobody wants this old doll," she said. She was talking to herself as much as to Dallas. "Not Miss Tate. Not even Quinn. That's what you do with stuff nobody wants, isn't it? You throw it away."

"Sure," Dallas said, though she seemed anything but sure.

It didn't feel quite right. But it was the only idea Jenna had. So she laid the doll on top of the garbage. The velvet dress and bonnet seemed to glow a deeper red against the white plastic. A curl of browning potato peel poked out of the slit in the top bag. It wrapped around the doll's arm.

Jenna shuddered and picked away the peel. Then, before she could change her mind, she lowered the lid.

Dallas gasped. "Are you really going to leave her there?" She said it as if they hadn't talked about it. As if she hadn't agreed.

"Of course." Jenna tried to sound more certain than she felt. It was just an old doll after all. A doll nobody wanted. What was the big deal? "Come on," she added, and she headed up the driveway. She tried to ignore the fact that Dallas wasn't following.

"Jenna," Dallas called. "Did you hear—"

"No!" Jenna interrupted. Her voice came out too loud. "I didn't hear anything." And she hadn't. She was certain she hadn't!

Dallas didn't reply. For once she must have decided not to argue. She started after Jenna.

That was when Quinn came around the corner of the garage. "Where is she?" she cried. "I heard her. What did you do with Miss Tate's doll?"

Dallas stopped again. "You heard the doll? What did you hear her say?"

"'Help me!'" Quinn said. She made her voice small and thin. "'Please, help me!'"

Dallas whirled to face Jenna. "That's what I heard, too," she said.

A shiver crawled up Jenna's spine. What

choice did she have? She ran back to the garbage can and lifted the lid.

When she picked the doll up, the blue eyes came open with a sharp clunk. This time Jenna could have sworn they were saying, *Gotcha!*

8
Gone!

"What are you going to do with her?" Dallas and Quinn said it in one breath. Then they both stood there, waiting for an answer. And Jenna hadn't even been the one who had wanted the doll in the first place!

It was Dallas who had told Miss Tate that Jenna wanted to buy the thing. It was Quinn who'd decided the doll was "full." But there they both stood, waiting for Jenna to do something. She looked down at the doll. The doll looked back at her.

And while Jenna stood there, staring right into the doll's eyes, she heard it. This time it wasn't a wail. It was a whisper, as soft as rustling leaves. But Jenna heard it perfectly.

"Help!" the doll begged. "Please, help me!"

Jenna jumped so violently the doll almost flew out of her hands. And even as she scrabbled to keep from dropping the thing, her hands were still trying to get rid of it.

She would have thrown it. She would have done exactly what her hands wanted except for one thing. Miss Tate. At that instant, their neighbor stepped out onto her front porch again. She came down the stairs and stood there on the other side of the street, her arms crossed, watching.

"Let's go!" Jenna cried. And holding the doll as far away from her body as possible, she began to run.

"Where?" Dallas asked.

Jenna didn't answer. She didn't know where. She just let her feet choose the path. And as if they knew no other place to go, her feet took her across the lawn . . . up the front steps . . . through the door . . . down

the hall . . . and into her room. Dallas and Quinn followed.

When she came through the door to her room, Jenna threw the doll. Hard. She couldn't help it. She had to be rid of the thing.

The doll landed on her bed, leaning crookedly against the headboard.

Jenna stepped back. Her breath stuttered and gasped. Had she heard Miss Tate's doll speak? Really?

If the doll had spoken, though, she said nothing now. She just sat there. Her round baby cheeks glowed, reflecting the red of the bonnet. Her blue eyes looked deep and knowing. They stared right at Jenna.

Suddenly a throaty wail pierced the air.

Jenna's hands flew to cover her ears. She stepped back, away from the doll, away from the noise.

But the noise only got louder.

Then she saw. The sound wasn't coming from the doll this time. It was coming from her cat. Rocco stood at the foot of the bed, howling!

Until that moment, Jenna hadn't noticed him curled in his usual place on her bed. But if his reaction had been strong when he saw the package that held the doll, it was even more violent now.

He didn't bother with hissing and spitting this time. Instead, a moaning growl came from his throat. His legs stiffened. His body went rigid. If he had been all black, he would have looked exactly like a Halloween cat. His head was low, his spine arched. He arched his tail, too, and laid back his ears.

He approached the doll sideways, crab-like.

"Don't, Rocco!" Quinn cried. She reached for the cat.

"Don't touch him!" Jenna warned. And in the same instant, Rocco's growl rose to a scream.

Row-w-w-w!

Quinn jerked her hand back.

They all stepped away from the bed, their gaze glued to the cat. Jenna put her arms around her little sister and held her close.

Rocco's yellow eyes were slits. Jenna had never seen her sweet cat look so mean.

Just when she couldn't stand the suspense
for another instant, Rocco sprang!

He swiped at the doll's face. His claws
caught in the lace edge of the bonnet. They
caught and held.

Rocco spat and hissed. He pulled his paw back. The doll tumbled toward him.

Rocco jerked harder. He yowled. He pulled the bonnet free. The doll rolled off the bed and hit the wooden floor with a loud *thwack!*

Rocco backed up. He shook his paw, dropping the bonnet onto the bed.

Once Rocco was free of the doll's bonnet, he stopped yowling. He crept back across the bed. Crouching, he peered over the side.

Jenna, Dallas, and Quinn moved around the bed to look, too. They all stood, staring at the fallen doll. A crack had opened across the top of her head. It ran from ear to ear.

"Oh," Quinn cried. "Look!"

Jenna looked. Something red was drifting through the crack in the doll's head. It seemed like red smoke.

At first the smoke had no shape. It was just a wisp, a curl. Then it began to take form. What was it?

Rocco yowled again.

"It's her!" Dallas cried.

Jenna didn't have to ask who Dallas meant by "her." Now she could see, too.

The red smoke had shaped itself into a girl. She wore a red-velvet dress, a red-velvet bonnet. Even her face was flushed red. And her hair was a bright coppery orange.

The red girl stayed joined to the broken doll at first. She didn't seem to know where to go. Then slowly, slowly she broke free. She

rose into the air. She floated toward the open window.

Rocco leapt to the floor and followed, moaning and keening the whole way.

"Shut the window!" Dallas cried.

But Quinn said, "No. Let her go!"

Jenna didn't move. She didn't think she could have stopped the gauzy figure if she had tried. And she didn't want to try.

Rocco had no such hesitation. As the wisp of a girl rose toward the open window, he leapt. His outstretched paw passed through the red mist. Then he was back on the floor, still howling.

And just like that . . . the red ghost was gone.

9

Hazel

Jenna stood in the doorway of Quinn's room, watching her play. Miss Tate's doll had joined Raggedy Ann and Barbie.

"Do you like your birthday present now?" Jenna asked.

Quinn picked up Miss Tate's old doll and hugged her. "I love her," she said. "Raggedy Ann and Barbie love her, too."

"So what have you named her?" Jenna

asked. And then—she didn't know why exactly—she held her breath.

"Shannon," Quinn replied. She held the doll out in front of her, smiling at it. "Her name is Shannon."

The breath Jenna had been holding leaked away. "Oh," she said. Was she disappointed? No, of course not. What was there to be disappointed about? Shannon was a perfectly good name. Perhaps it was even too good for an old doll with a cracked-and-glued head.

Still, she couldn't help saying it. "Are you sure it's Shannon? Not something more . . . well, old-fashioned?"

Quinn shook her head. She walked Shannon over to Barbie and sat her down at the tiny doll's side. "No," she said. "She's Shannon now. Hazel is gone."

Jenna drew in her breath. She had never said anything to Quinn about Hazel. "Who told you that?" she asked. "About the girl? About Hazel?"

Now Quinn walked Raggedy Ann over to join the others. "Hazel did." She said it in a voice that implied, *Of course!* or even, *Who do you think, dummy?*

Jenna wanted to ask more questions. All kinds of questions. But she didn't know where to begin. So she just stood there, watching Quinn play.

"She said, 'Thank you,'" Quinn said finally.

What are you talking about? Jenna

thought. But she asked, "Do you mean Hazel?" She said the name lightly. She tried to make it sound perfectly ordinary for little girls to get messages from other little girls who were long dead.

"Hazel," Quinn agreed. "She wanted out. For a long, long time, she wanted out. So she said, 'Thank you.'"

"Who was she thanking?" Jenna asked.

"You," Quinn said. "Maybe Rocco, too. She was just happy. Happy to go, you know?"

Jenna nodded. She shifted her weight from one foot to the other. Dallas was waiting for her. They were going to ride bikes this morning. But she had another question, just one more. She had to know.

"Where did Hazel go?" she asked.

"Away," Quinn answered. She looked up from her dolls for the first time as she said it and smiled at Jenna. "She went away." Somehow, she made "away" sound like a very pleasant place.

Jenna sighed. She didn't know why she was relieved, but she was. She didn't know why she trusted Quinn's answer, either, but she did.

What she did know for certain was that she was happy for Hazel.

Very happy.

Should she tell Miss Tate?

No, she didn't think so. There were some things it was probably better for grown-ups not to know.

"Well," she said. "I've got to go."

"Say goodbye to the dolls," ordered Quinn.

So Jenna did. "Bye, Raggedy Ann. Bye, Barbie. Bye, Shannon." And she wiggled her fingers at them in a tiny wave.

Bye, Hazel, she added, though only in her thoughts.

Still, she couldn't help but be relieved, all over again, when the doll in the red-velvet dress didn't reply.

About the Author

Marion Dane Bauer is the author of more than sixty books for children, including the Newbery Honor–winning *On My Honor*. She has also won the Kerlan Award for her collected work. Marion's first Stepping Stone book, *The Blue Ghost,* was named to the Texas Bluebonnet Award 2007–2008 Master List. Marion teaches writing and is on the faculty of the Vermont College Master of Fine Arts in Writing for Children and Young Adults program.

Marion has two grown children and seven grandchildren and lives in Eden Prairie, Minnesota.

About the Illustrator

Peter Ferguson has illustrated such books as the Sisters Grimm series, the Lucy Rose series, and *The Anybodies* and its sequels, and he has painted the covers for many others. He lives in Montreal with his wife, Eriko, and cat, Yoda.